Prince Boghole

Erik Christian Haugaard

illustrations by Julie Downing

Macmillan Publishing Company   New York

For Patricia
–E. H.

To Scott, Peter, and Jeffrey
–J. D.

Macmillan Publishing Company, 866 Third Avenue, New York, N.Y. 10022   Collier Macmillan Canada, Inc.

Printed and bound in Japan

First American Edition 10 9 8 7 6 5 4 3 2 1

The text of this book is set in 16 point Cloister. The illustrations are rendered in watercolor.

Library of Congress Cataloging-in-Publication Data   Haugaard, Erik Christian. Prince Boghole. Summary: Desmond, ruler of a
kingdom on the island of Eire, promises his daughter's hand to the prince who brings him the most wonderful bird.
[1. Fairy tales. 2. Ireland – Fiction] I. Downing, Julie, ill. II. Title.
PZ8.H2934Pr   1987   [E]   86-61   ISBN 0-02-743440-0

Once long, long ago the kingdom of Munster on the island of Eire was ruled by a king named Desmond. He had but one child, a girl named Orla. For many years the king had been a widower and his daughter had been brought up by her nurse, Gormlai. Gormlai was so wise that she had wisdom to spare and, though she loved the girl, she had not spoiled her. The princess was as good as she was beautiful, and that is rare, especially among princesses.

Now, the king had reached the age when even a golden crown rests heavily on the head, so he called his daughter to him and said, "Soon a spring will come when I shall not watch the salmon return to the rivers, nor see the grass sprout and clothe the hills in green; therefore, it is my desire to see you married to a prince who will not shame my crown. I have sent messages to the kings of Leinster and Ulster, asking each to send one of his sons, and you shall choose between them. I have said that they should not send their oldest sons, for their hearts would ever be at home, nor their youngest, for the youngest ones are always spoiled."

"When will they come?" asked Princess Orla.

"As fast as their horses can carry them," said King Desmond with a laugh, "for princes are as eager to become kings as the gray cygnets are to be swans."

At that moment someone knocked at the door of the castle, and a servant was sent down to open it.

The visitor said that his name was Brian, and he claimed to be a prince, but he didn't look like one. His clothes were made of homespun cloth, and on his head he wore a knitted cap with a bright feather in it.

"Where would your father's kingdom be?" King Desmond asked, while he eyed the prince's sword, which looked as if the village blacksmith had made it.

"Across the mountains, to the northwest, where the big waves break against the shore. His kingdom is poor and I have six brothers. That is why I have set out to have a look at the world and, if it pleases me, to carve a corner of it for my own."

The young man took off his cap and bowed to the king and Princess Orla. His hair fell loose to his shoulders and was as black as a raven's wing.

His hair pleases me, thought the princess.

His speech pleases me, thought King Desmond.

But all of the servants tittered softly, and one of them whispered, "His father's kingdom is a bog, only good for cutting turf. Let's call him Prince Boghole."

"You cannot be the oldest son, for then your father would have kept you home; but are you the youngest?" King Desmond asked, for, like most people, he was slow to give up an idea.

"I have three brothers who are older and three who are younger. The youngest of them is still a lad, and my mother would sooner part with all of the rest of us than lose him."

No answer could have pleased the king more, and he bade Prince Brian welcome.

The next day the son of the King of Leinster arrived. His hair was as golden as Princess Orla's. Each of his ten attendants was more splendidly dressed than King Desmond, which didn't please the king, but he didn't show it.

Then came the Prince of Ulster with twenty retainers, all heavily armed. On his right shoulder sat a falcon. The bird looked at Princess Orla with cold, yellow eyes; and that did not please the princess.

Now, thirty-three guests will crowd any table and empty even a royal larder, so it was not long before the king asked his daughter which of the princes she would like as a husband.

"The Prince of Leinster loves his clothes too much," Princess Orla answered, and her father smiled. He liked his old clothes best and wore his crown only when he had to.

"Then you will marry the Prince of Ulster?" he asked.

"His eyes are like his falcon's: cold and hard," she replied.

"You will have to choose between them." King Desmond scowled, for he did not fancy either as a son-in-law.

"What about Prince Brian?" the princess asked slowly.

Her father shook his head. He had heard what the servants had dubbed the young man, and he could not give his daughter's hand to someone called Prince Boghole.

"I would send them all away," Gormlai, who had been listening, advised. "If they stay we shall have to slaughter the milk cows, and then what shall we do for cheese? Let them perform some feat to win Orla. Who has ever heard of a princess being given away like a shepherd's daughter?"

"That would have done in my grandfather's time, when there were still a few giants left, and even a dragon or two in Dingle," said the king. "But what could one ask them to do these days?"

"Let them travel for a year and each bring back that bird he thinks most wonderful; then we can decide which fowl is fairest, and his master shall have the princess." Gormlai smiled, turned and was gone, for she knew that her back had won many an argument.

By noon the next day the king had put away his crown and was wearing his woolen nightcap. The princess's favorite cat had had kittens in the drawer where she kept her second-best clothes, and everything was peaceful once more.

Princess Orla dreamed every night of Prince Brian with the raven locks; her father had a cape made that was black as night on one side and blue as midday on the other. He felt certain that no one in Leinster had any that was finer.

Although a year is long, it is soon gone. Gormlai saw to it that all the bedrooms in the castle had been aired and there was food enough for an army.

The first to return was the Prince of Leinster. This time he had twenty attendants and they were even more splendidly dressed. He, himself, wore a cloak that shone on one side like the moon and, on the other, like the sun.

"Father-in-law," he said, "our cloaks are a perfect match: Yours is the sky and mine that which glitters and shines in it."

This speech did not please King Desmond. He thought, *Father-in-law, indeed!*

Next came the Prince of Ulster. Forty men on horseback rode behind him and their spears were tipped with silver.

Now Prince Brian must come, thought Princess Orla. Five times a day she ran to the top of the tower to look for him, but all she saw were the yellow gorse bushes and the grazing sheep.

When five days had passed, the two princes demanded that Princess Orla decide which of them had brought back the more remarkable bird. While the Prince of Ulster spoke, his forty men shook their spears; that was a tradition in Ulster.

King Desmond did not think much of such a custom, but he agreed that after the banquet that night his daughter would choose which prince she would marry.

Princess Orla, who did not want to marry either of them, got a headache and, when that didn't help, she burst into tears and swore she would die.

"You have made your bed; now you must lie in it," her father said, which was not true, for it was he who had made it, but that he had forgotten.

The banquet was a splendid affair, but the princess could hardly eat a bite, even of the dessert.

"Bring in my bird," commanded the Prince of Ulster. "Far to the north did I travel, to the country of steep mountains and deep forests. There, on the highest peak, I found and conquered this, the king of birds."

Two of his soldiers entered the hall, carrying a thick branch between them. On it sat an eagle so fierce that even the bravest of the guests were pleased to see that its feet were shackled with a golden chain.

"A fine bird," said King Desmond. "But I think you will find that here in Munster both our rabbits and our mountains are too small for it."

Then he turned to the Prince of Leinster and asked to see the bird he had brought.

"I have sailed to the south, to the country where even the milkmaids have manners and the royal palace is so large that no one can count its rooms. There, for its weight in Irish gold, I have bought this, the most beautiful of birds."

The prince nodded, and one of his attendants brought into the hall a peacock. It spread its tail, which looked like a wheel on God's chariot. The servants all hoped that their princess would choose the son of the King of Leinster.

Everyone looked at the princess, and she looked at the two birds. The eagle with its fiery eyes frightened her, but the peacock had the head of a hen and stupid, beady eyes. Gormlai, who was standing next to the princess, whispered something in her ear and the girl asked if the birds could sing.

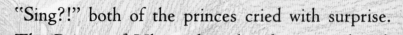

"Sing?!" both of the princes cried with surprise.

The Prince of Ulster drew his dagger and with its sharp point tickled the eagle. The great bird shrieked in fury, so loudly that it could be heard a mile away. "Thus does an eagle sing," he said, and looked as if he could shriek as wildly himself.

No sooner had the eagle grown quiet than the peacock started to cackle in fright. Its high voice sounded like a madman's laughter.

Everyone looked at the bird, in wonder that anything so lovely could have so foul a voice. The peacock must have felt its shame, for the bird folded its great tail.

At that moment, unnoticed by all except Princess Orla, young Prince Brian entered. "And what bird have you brought?" she asked, full of hope.

The young prince looked a bit the worse for his traveling; he had journeyed most of the way on foot. In his left hand he carried a stick and, in his right, a wicker basket.

"I have sailed east to the country where the cliffs are low and the waters warm. There, in the woods, I caught this bird." Then he drew from its cage a tiny, colorless bird.

"It is uglier than a sparrow," whispered the servants. Princess Orla almost wept; how could she choose such a drab little creature over the eagle or the peacock?

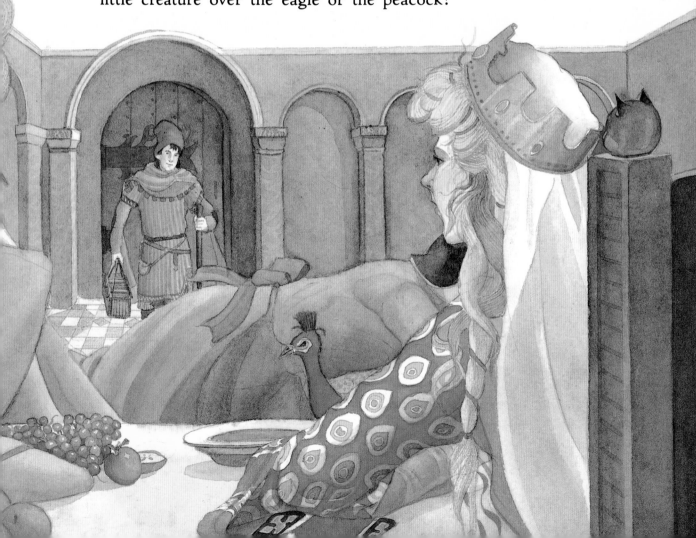

Prince Brian stroked the bird's head gently and sat it on top of his staff. For a moment the tiny creature looked around, and then it started to sing. So beautiful was its song that everyone in the hall forgot the peacock and the eagle and, almost, themselves.

"That is the most marvelous of birds!" Princess Orla proclaimed, and even the servants declared that it looked most distinguished.

The Prince of Ulster grew angry and left with his forty men without saying good-bye. The Prince of Leinster told everyone that life in the country was not for him, and took his peacock and went back to his great city.

The wedding feast of Princess Orla and Prince Brian lasted a week, and even the kitchen maids and the boy who turned the spit had as much to eat as they had ever dreamed of.

The nightingale flew away, and no one has ever seen or heard a nightingale in Munster since. But that didn't bother Prince Brian, for he came from the west country, and there they like to do the singing themselves.